UK edition printed by UK Comics - www.ukcomicscreative.co.uk
US edition printed by Quick Comics - www.quickcomics.com

ISBN: 978-1-909276-09-3

ATOMIC ★ SHEEP

written and illustrated by
sally jane thompson

edited by
sara westrop

for markosia enterprises ltd

HARRY MARKOS
publisher & managing partner

IAN SHARMAN ■ GM JORDAN ■ TOBY SHORT
group editors

ANDY BRIGGS
creative consultant

AAM/MARKOSIA

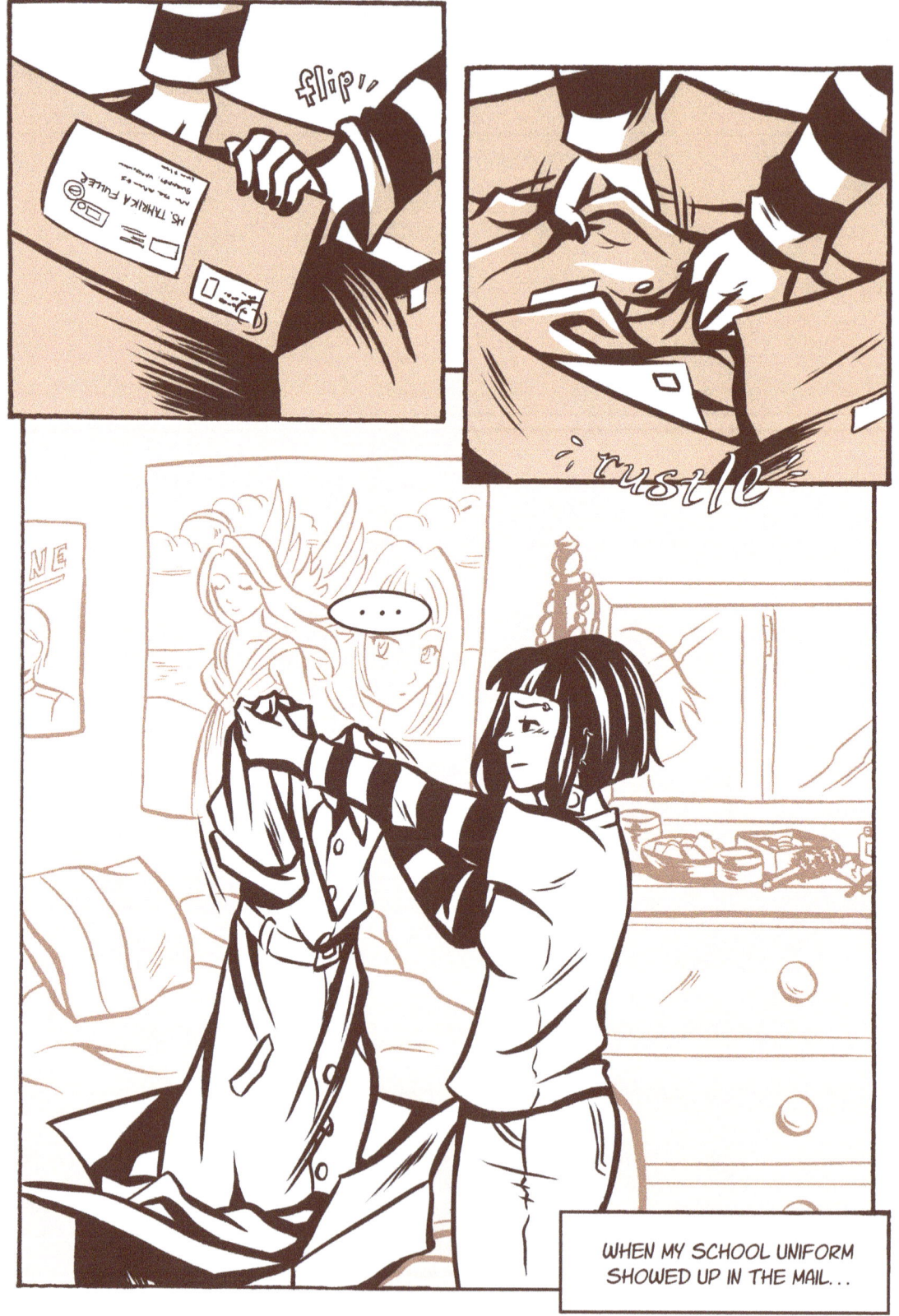

THEY STARTED CUTTING BACK ON SOME STUFF A COUPLE OF YEARS AGO. LIKE, THEIR OWN STUFF - MOM'S HAIR APPOINTMENTS AND STUFF.

...YES, I'M AFRAID I'LL HAVE TO CANCEL MY APPOINTMENT FOR THURSDAY...

?

GOLF? OH, NOT THIS WEEK. I'M JUST TAKING A LITTLE BREAK FOR A WHILE.

PENGUINS ATTACK

THE DAILY PLAN

SO I DIDN'T EVEN *THINK* ABOUT THE SCHOOL THING, 'CAUSE I THOUGHT MONEY WAS TIGHT.

BUT THEN THEY TELL ME...

WE'VE BEEN PUTTING MONEY ASIDE FOR A COUPLE OF YEARS, SO YOU CAN DO GRADE 11 AND 12 THERE!

yaaay...

OH.

...CRAP.

YEAH.

hool Rules, 20

...s of conduct, all grades:

...at all times with respect. T...

...t when teachers is sp...

...intaining a pro...

...times.

Piercings:

Female students may wear a maximum of two studs per ear. No other piercings permitted.

MAN! I'LL HAVE TO JUST PUT THEM IN OVERNIGHT, TO KEEP THE HOLES FROM CLOSING...

OH, *WHAT?!* "NO UNNATURAL HAIR COLOURS PERMITTED"?

BEEP.

sigh

DUN DUN DUN

COLOUR • DEVELOPER

LUSTRE

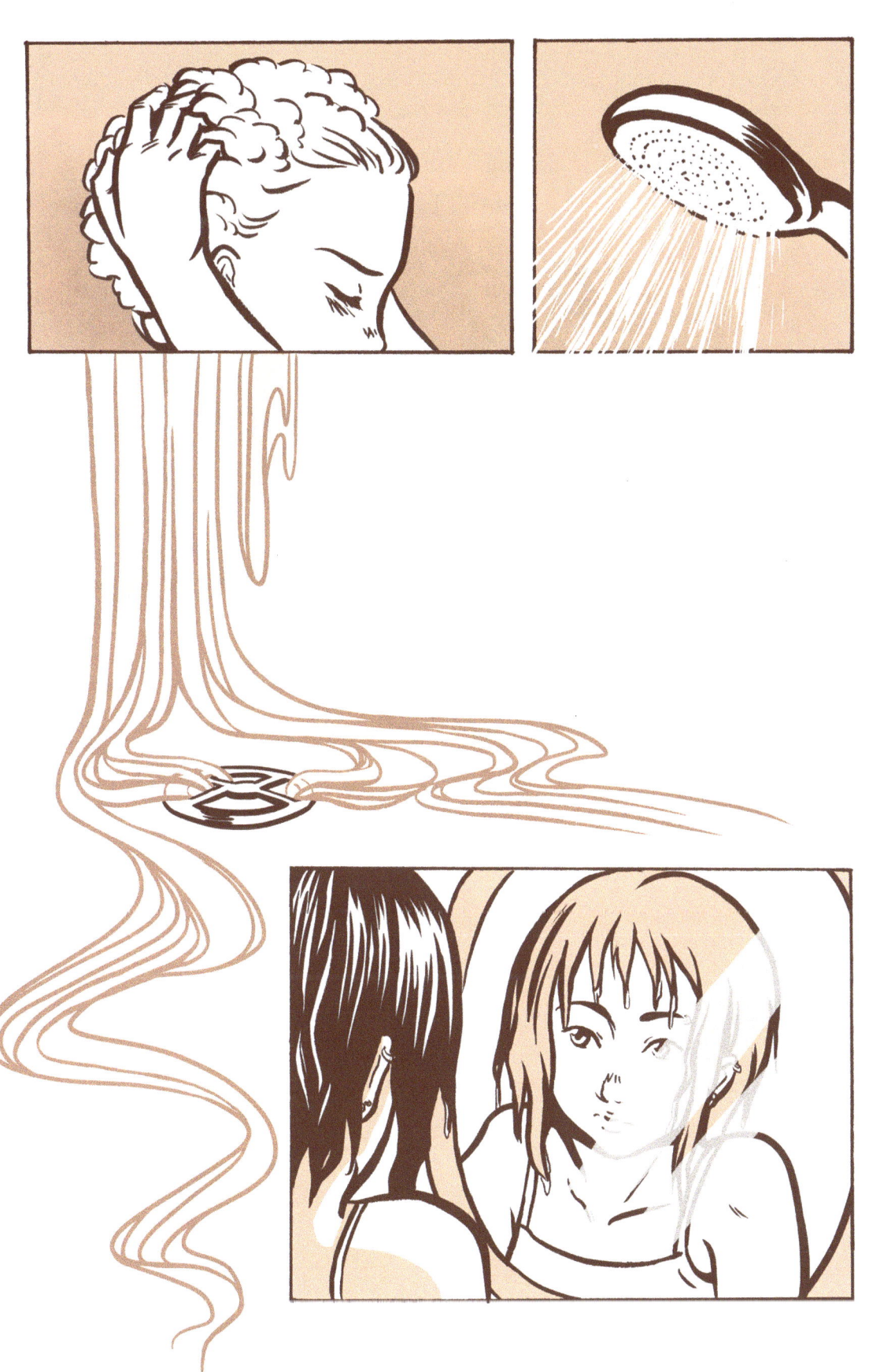

OKAY, I'LL ADMIT - THE FOREST OUT HERE IS REALLY, REALLY GORGEOUS.

STILL, THERE'S, LIKE, *NOTHING* OUT HERE...

"SIGH"

OKAY, THAT'S...
KINDA COOL.

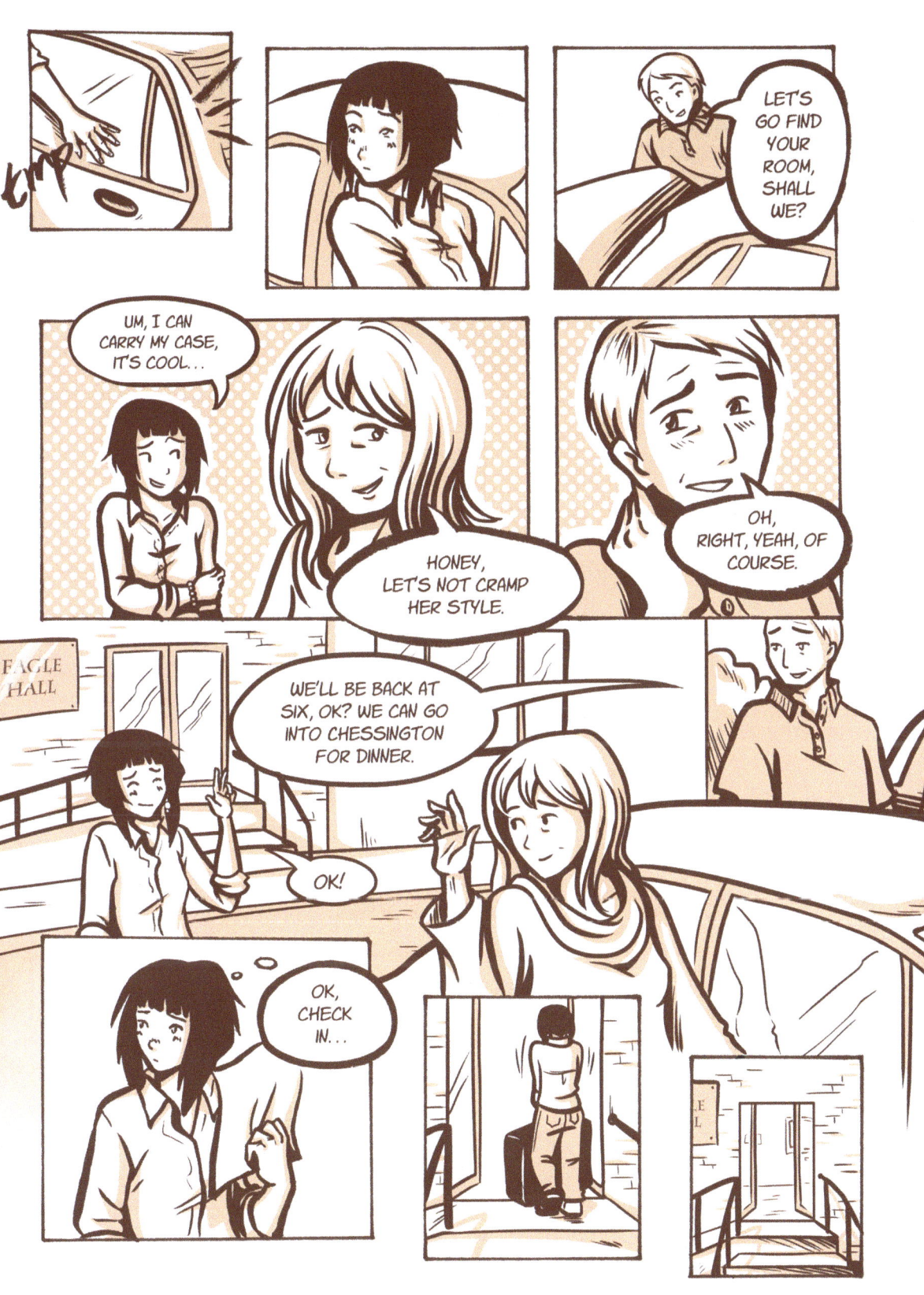

I'M...
...STUCK HERE FOREVER. THERE'S NO WAY OUT!
WHICH DOOR DO I GO THROUGH?!
OK, OK. HERE GOES ...

Creeak

GLARE

BEEP!
BEEP!

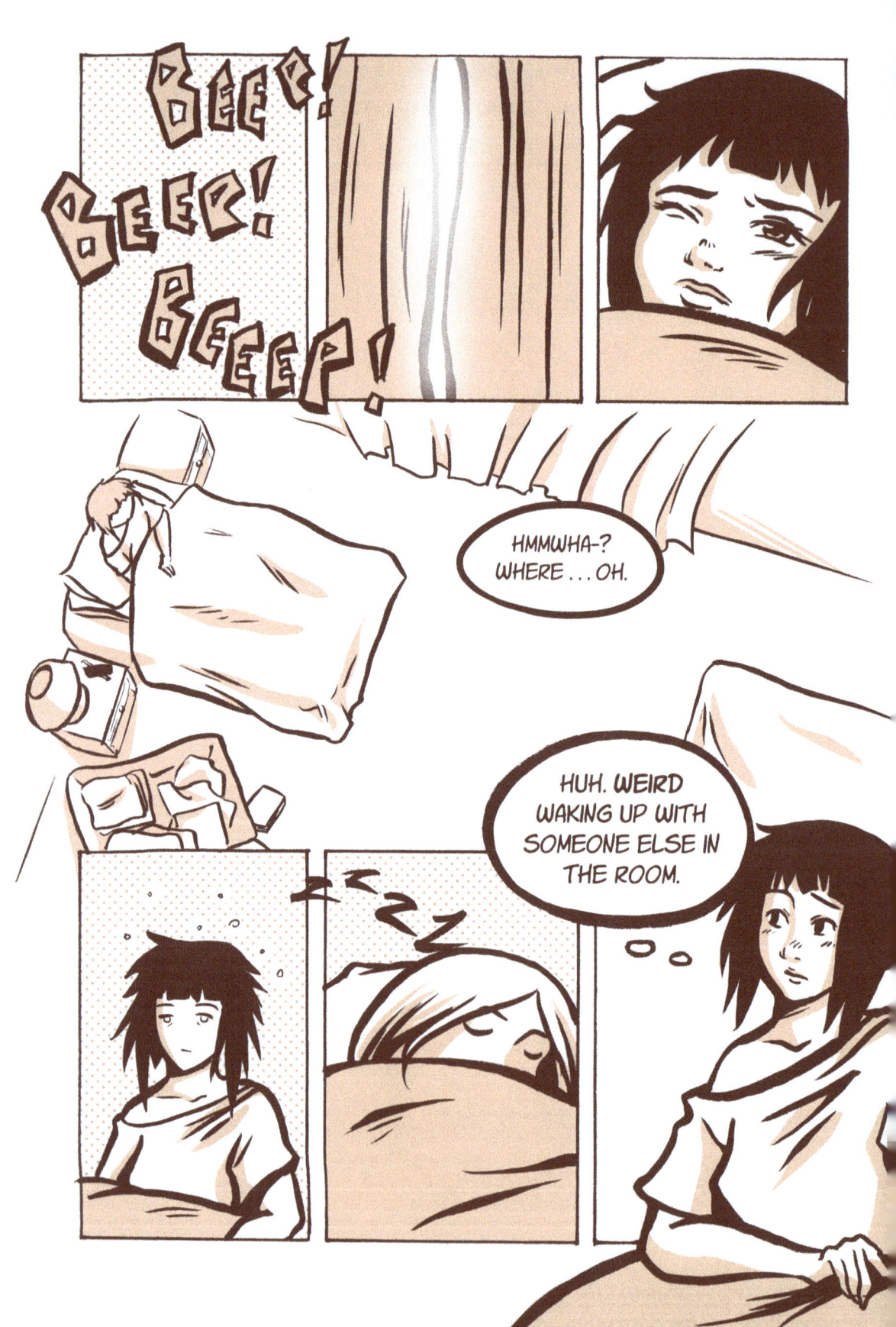

FIRST DAY.

WOOSH

WOOSH

AH, GUY'S UNIFORM HUH?

YEEEAAH. THE HANDBOOK SAID IT'S ALLOWED, RIGHT?

WELL, IT'S ALLOWED, YEAH...

?

THIS SCHOOL JUST... ISN'T NON-CONFORMIST CENTRAL, THAT'S ALL.

I SEE YOU GOT DRESSED IN YOUR GRANDMOTHER'S WARDROBE, AS USUAL!

WOAH.

YEP, I LIKE IT IN THERE. AND I SEE YOU ALL GOT DRESSED IN A CLONING MACHINE, AS USUAL.

WOAH!

UGH, WHATEVER. WHO'S THIS, NEW BOYFRIEND? RYAN FINALLY SEE SENSE?

...WHAT THE HADES, BECKY. THIS IS MY NEW ROOMMATE, TAMRIKA.

...

O...OF COURSE I KNEW, UH, I WAS JUST KIDDING! ER, SORRY.

MAYBE YOU SHOULD HEAD TO ASSEMBLY, BEFORE YOU EMBARRASS YOURSELF FURTHER?

YOU MEAN, BEFORE I EMBARRASS YOU?

SURE, BECKY.

..."HOME", HUH?

chapter 2

UM, I'M TAMRIKA... UH, TAMMY.

THEY'RE ALL MATH AND SCIENCE JOBS!

MAYBE.. AN, UH ILLUSTRATOR? OR GRAPHIC DESIGNER OR SOMETHING...

WAIT, WHY DO I SOUND LIKE I'M APOLOGIZING?

JASMINE.

A PULITZER WINNING NOVELIST.

TWEET!

TWEET!

WELL, UM, ALWAYS GOOD TO BE AMBITIOUS! AND, UH, CONFIDENT... WHO'S NEXT?

"CONFIDENT", NO KIDDING!

COOL THOUGH! I WISH I WAS THAT SURE.

SssSh

ROOM 21A

OOH, CONDOLENCES. HE *IS* *RIDICULOUSLY* DULL.

OH, MAN, YOU GOT ARNOLD?

HERE, TEA OF THE DAY.

HMM . . . NOT BAD! KINDA . . . SMOKY?

WHAT IS IT?

GENMAICHA.

SOUNDS NICE.

. . .

Sigh

WOULD YOU LIKE SOME?

ha ha!

OOH, YES PLEASE! THAT'D BE GREAT!

WHAT AM I DOING?

A SHED?

BETTER STOP THE DETECTIVE ROUTINE HERE.

OH, HEY!

!!CAUGHT!!

eek!

YOU'RE THE GIRL I RAN INTO! UH, SORRY 'BOUT THAT.

UM, I...

WERE YOU... STEALING... PAINT?

MAYBE, UM... BORROWING? HEH.

LOOK, COULD YOU JUST... COME LOOK INSIDE, BEFORE YOU TELL ON ME?

SO HOW COME YOU'RE STEALING PAINT AND DOING THIS ON YOUR OWN?
"BORROWING"!
HAVE YOU HAD AN ART CLASS YET?
YEAH. OKAY, I SEE WHAT YOU MEAN.
YEAH, THIS IS A REALLY CRAPPY SCHOOL FOR ME. I'M ONLY HERE CAUSE MY DAD WORKS HERE.
OH. WHAT'S HE DO?
GROUNDSKEEPING STUFF.
OH, THAT'S WHY YOU HAVE THAT SHED?
YEAH.
I'M ONLY HERE BECAUSE MY PARENTS WANTED ME TO COME, REALLY.
I'M TAMRIKA BY THE WAY. TAMMY.
I'M JAKE.
BLAH BLAH
BLAH BLAH!
BLAH BLAH BLAH
BLAH
BLAH
BLAH

CLICK

WRITING?

COOL, MY SKETCHBOOK'S STILL IN HERE!

SSSSh

THIS PLACE IS PRETTY SPECIAL.

MAYBE I CAN BE HAPPY HERE. IT HAS ITS GOOD POINTS, OBVIOUSLY.

MAYBE...

THE REST OF IT COULD BE GOOD TOO?

HEY JAZZ?

MM?

WAIT, JAZZ?

OH! I'M SORRY, I SHOULD'VE-

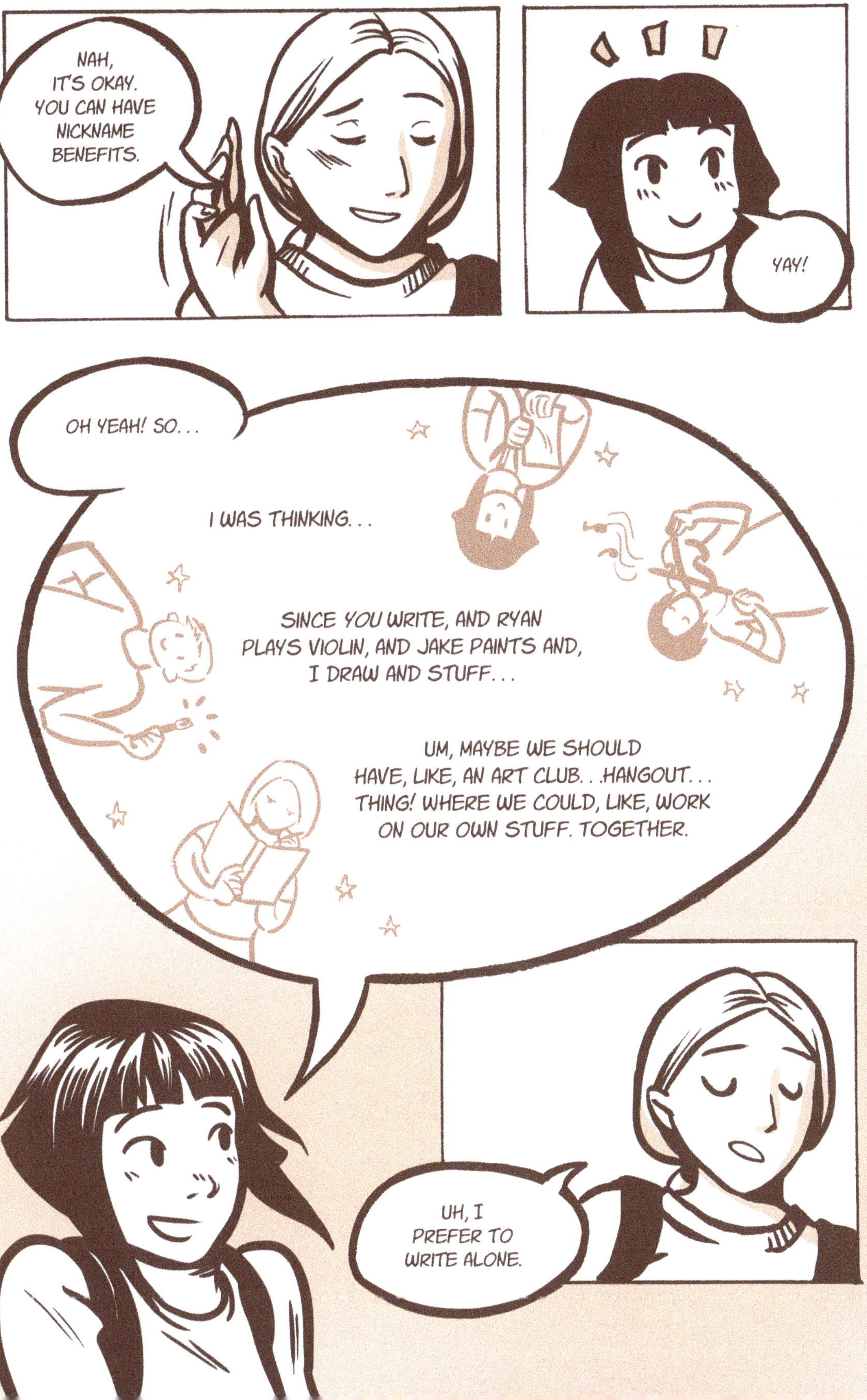

NAH, IT'S OKAY. YOU CAN HAVE NICKNAME BENEFITS.

YAY!

OH YEAH! SO...

I WAS THINKING...

SINCE YOU WRITE, AND RYAN PLAYS VIOLIN, AND JAKE PAINTS AND, I DRAW AND STUFF...

UM, MAYBE WE SHOULD HAVE, LIKE, AN ART CLUB...HANGOUT... THING! WHERE WE COULD, LIKE, WORK ON OUR OWN STUFF. TOGETHER.

UH, I PREFER TO WRITE ALONE.

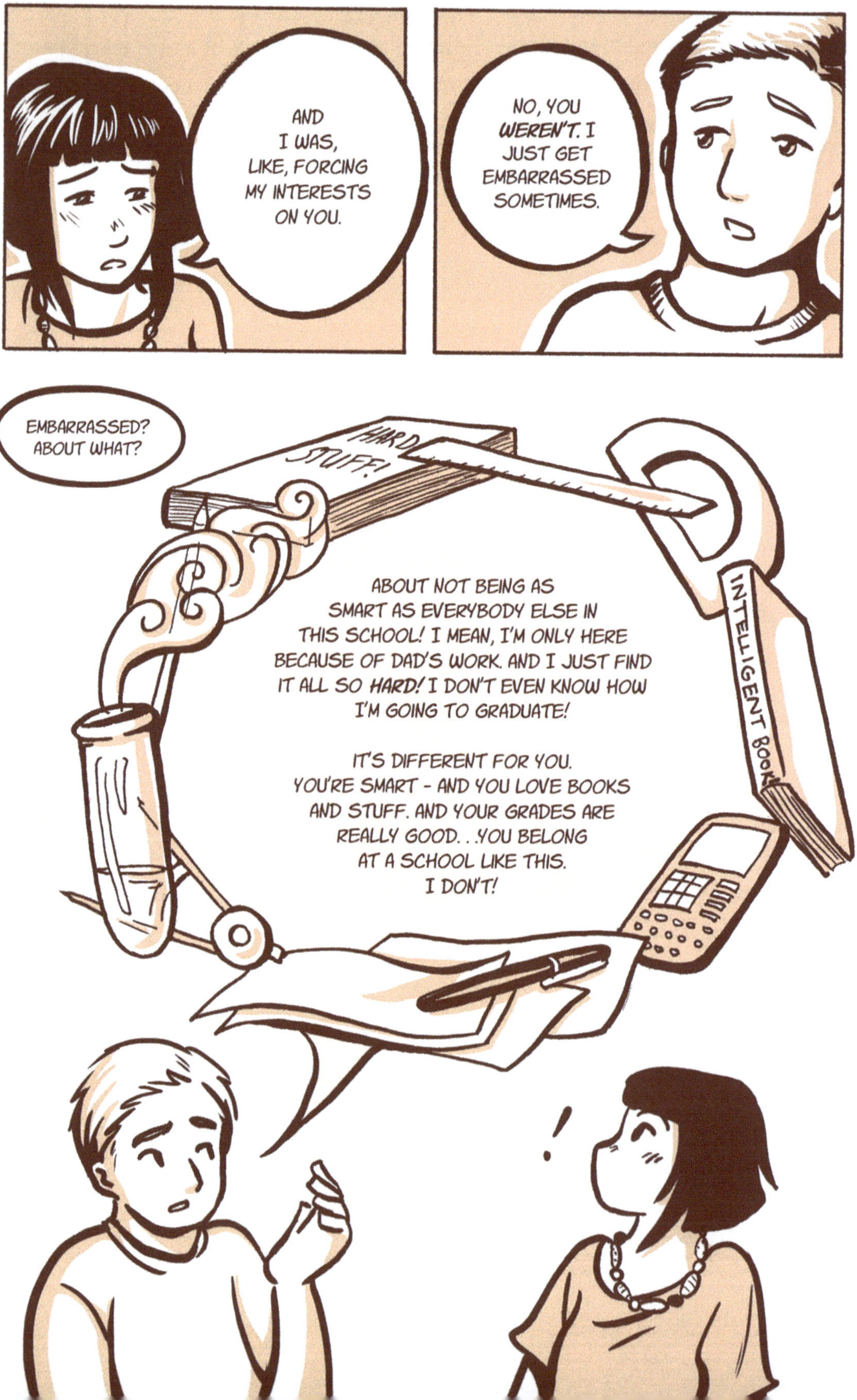

chapter 3

AND I WAS, LIKE, FORCING MY INTERESTS ON YOU.

NO, YOU *WEREN'T.* I JUST GET EMBARRASSED SOMETIMES.

EMBARRASSED? ABOUT WHAT?

ABOUT NOT BEING AS SMART AS EVERYBODY ELSE IN THIS SCHOOL! I MEAN, I'M ONLY HERE BECAUSE OF DAD'S WORK. AND I JUST FIND IT ALL *SO HARD!* I DON'T EVEN KNOW HOW I'M GOING TO GRADUATE!

IT'S DIFFERENT FOR YOU. YOU'RE SMART - AND YOU LOVE BOOKS AND STUFF. AND YOUR GRADES ARE REALLY GOOD. . .YOU BELONG AT A SCHOOL LIKE THIS. I DON'T!

HARD STUFF!

INTELLIGENT BOOK

I JUST WANNA DRAW!

SIGH. I SAY THAT. BUT.

THIS IS SO CLICHÉ!

I'VE GOT NO STYLE.

JAKE'S PAINTINGS ARE SO TEXTUREY AND INTERESTING.

MAYBE I SHOULD DO SCIENCE OR SOMETHING AT UNI...

AGH! STUPID BECKY, WHAT IS HER *PROBLEM?!*

CARE TO ELABORATE?

WE SHOULD HAVE SENT SOMEONE ELSE WITH THE CLUB APPLICATION. I'M 100% SURE SHE'S JUST DOING IT TO SPITE ME.

SUPPOSEDLY YOU NOW NEED *TEN MEMBERS* AND A FACULTY SPONSOR, BEFORE YOU CAN REGISTER AS A CLUB AND USE SCHOOL FACILITIES, OR GET ANY CLUB FUNDING.

I'M SURE IT'LL BE EASY! I MEAN, YOU'RE SO POPULAR, WITH THAT CHARMING PERSONALITY!

:Snrk!:

THE STAMP CLUB HAS _TWO_ MEMBERS.

PRE-EXISTING CLUB.

WOW. WHAT DID YOU *DO* TO THIS GIRL?
OH, THANK YOU! I LOVE HOW YOU ASSUME IT'S MY FAULT.
WE USED TO BE FRIENDS WHEN WE WERE YOUNGER.
UNTIL SHE DECIDED SHE'D RATHER BE FASHION-Y AND POPULAR. I MEAN, YOU KNOW HOW IT GOES.
IS THERE ANY CHANCE YOU GUYS COULD'VE JUST MISUNDERSTOOD EACH OTHER?
UH, NO.

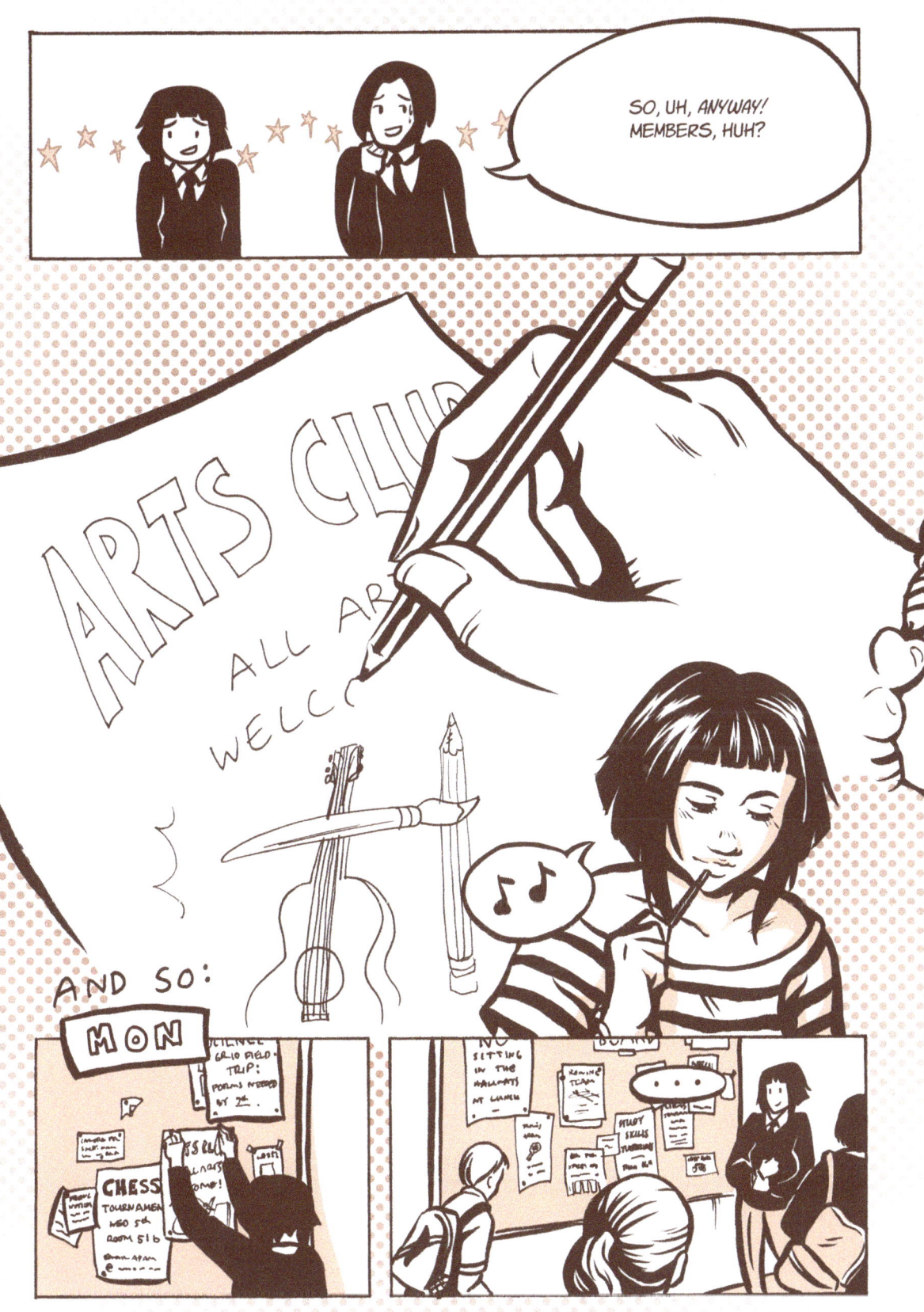

DON'T WORRY.

YOU JUST NEED TO FIND YOUR VOICE, IS ALL.

OH, IS THAT ALL?

UM, I KNOW THAT'S PROBABLY NOT VERY HELPFUL.

WHAT DO I KNOW ANYWAY?

I MEAN, I JUST PAINT WHAT LOOKS GOOD TO ME, REALLY!

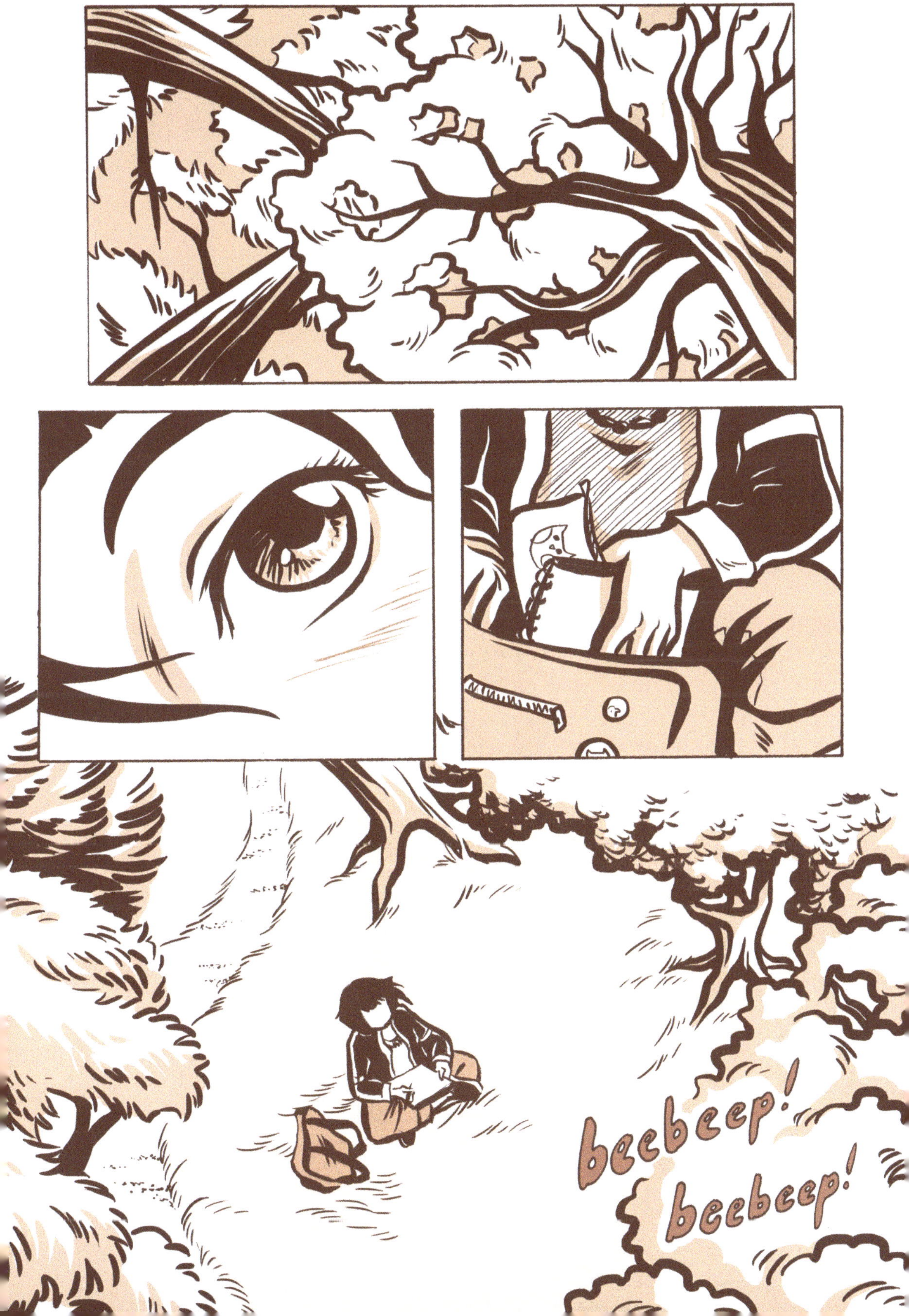

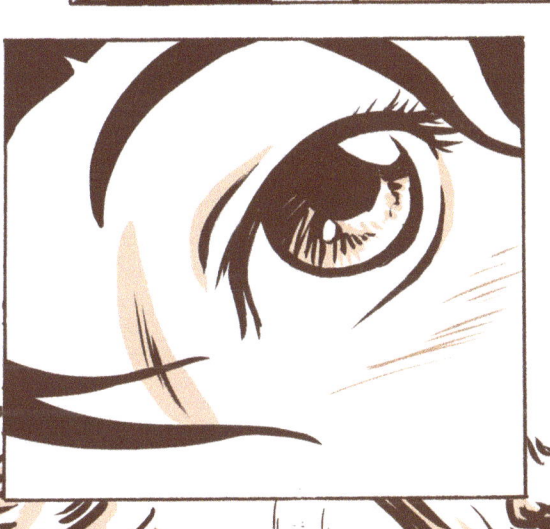

beebeep!
beebeep!

HOW DID YOU AND RYAN...
I MEAN, WHEN DID YOU KNOW YOU HAD, LIKE, A CONNECTION, OR...
YOU KNOW WHAT I MEAN, RIGHT?
?
HUH. WELL, I HAD A LIST IN MY HEAD OF THINGS I'D WANT IN A GUY...

AN INTERESTING CONVERSATIONALIST... SOMEONE I CAN TALK TO ABOUT LITERATURE, POLITICS, ART, PHILOSOPHY... THAT WAY WE'D NEVER BORE EACH OTHER... SOMEONE INTERESTED IN THE WORLD, IN TRAVEL... NOT A STEREOTYPICAL MACHO GUY, OR WORRIED ABOUT MEETING STEREOTYPES LIKE THAT... MAYBE INTERESTED IN SOME SORT OF CREATIVE OR CULTURALLY-RELATED CAREER... PREFERABLY SOMEONE WHO LIKES WORDS AND LANGUAGE AND WON'T GET "YOUR" AND "YOU'RE" MIXED UP... SOMEONE CALM... I DON'T REALLY HAVE ANY LOOKS PREFERENCES, BUT SOMEONE WHO TAKES CARE OF HIMSELF... HMM, WHAT ELSE?...

RYAN AND I ARE INTELLECTUAL EQUALS. WE'RE A GOOD MATCH.

HMM.

BUT!

YOU AND JAKE HAVE A LOT IN COMMON, PERSONALITY-WISE AT LEAST. YOU'RE DEFINITELY BOTH JANE AND BINGLEY TYPES!

LA.

chapter 4

I KINDA WISH PEOPLE'D SHORTEN IT TO *RIKA* INSTEAD. THAT'D BE RAD.

OKAY!

HUH?

CLICK

I COULD CALL YOU THAT! NOT THE SAME AS *EVERYONE*, BUT...

...MAYBE STILL SOMETHING COOL ABOUT JUST ONE PERSON USING IT? LIKE SECRET CODE!

RYAN AND JAZZ NOT COMING TODAY?

NAH.

AH, COUPLE TIME!

THEY'RE REALLY GOOD TOGETHER, AREN'T THEY?

MMHMM!

HMM. . .

?

YOU DON'T THINK SO?

I DUNNO, I JUST KIND OF GET THIS FEELING OF... DISTANCE?... BETWEEN THEM.

RYAN...

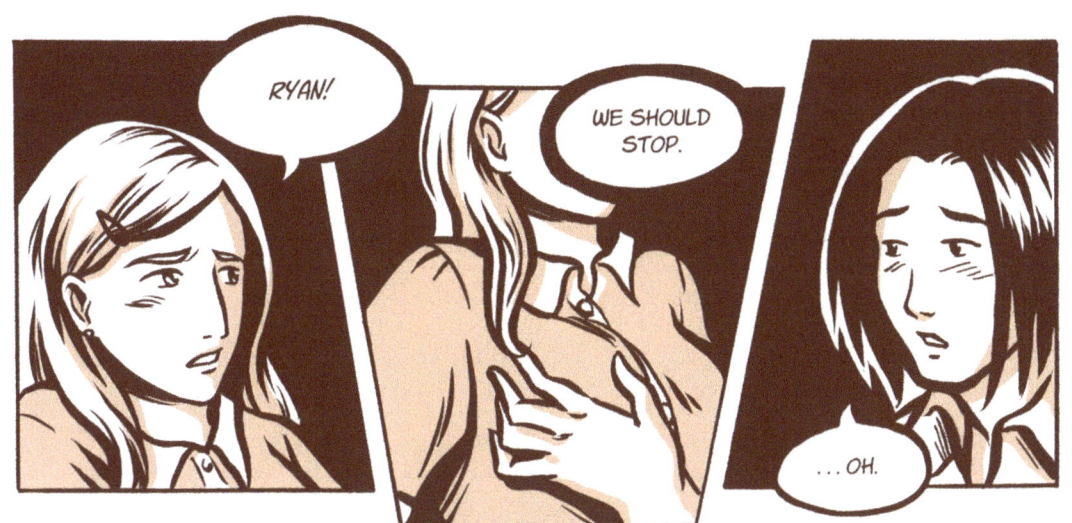

TODAY YOU'LL CARRY ON WITH MORE, ER, PERSPECTIVE PRACTICE.

grooooan!

AW, MAN!

DETERMINATION!

NO, COME ON TAMMY!

sigh

I'M GONNA GET SOMETHING OUT OF THIS!

C'MON JAZZ, PLEASE.

I LOVE YOU.

...I LOVE YOU TOO RYAN.

THEN-

BUT YOU KNOW I'M JUST NOT READY YET.

I'M STARTING TO THINK YOU NEVER WILL BE!

I MEAN, IF YOU REALLY LOVED ME, WOULDN'T YOU WANT TO BE WITH ME?

HEY RYAN!

HUH?

JAZZ?

chk

snff

snff

OH, UM, SORRY, I-

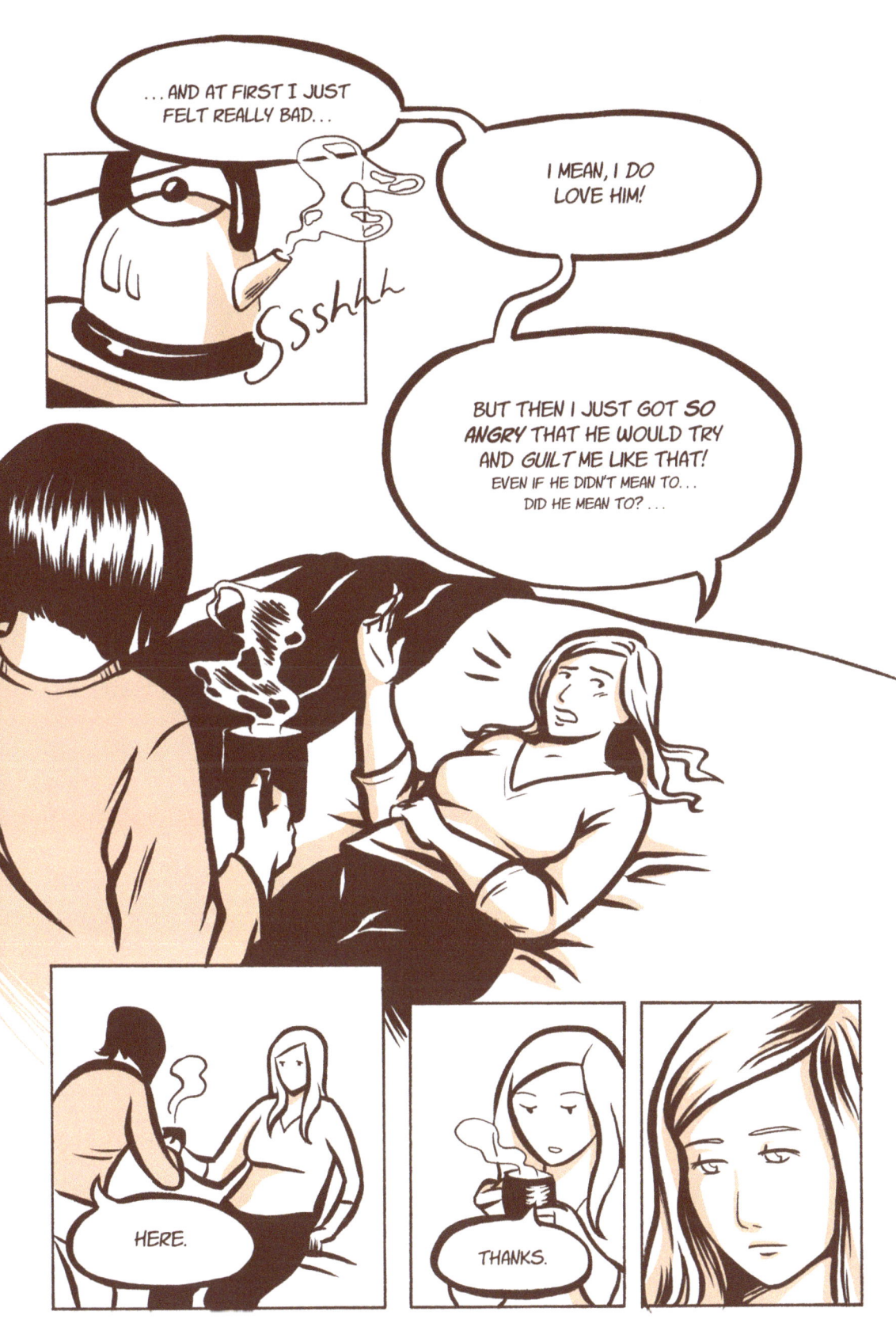

chapter 5

DING
DING!

IT'S SO
BEAUTIFUL!

SO! ONE
SEMESTER DOWN!
WHAT'DYA THINK . . . GLAD
YOU CAME IN THE END?

. . . OR NOT
SO MUCH?

HMM.

WRRRRRr.!

RrRRR

OH! HIEYJAZZ.

HMM? OH. HI BECKY.

I, UH, I HEARD ABOUT YOU AND RYAN. ...

HOW ON *EARTH* DO PEOPLE HEAR ABOUT THESE THINGS?

: *sigh* : WHATEVER.

YOU MUST BE HAPPY, AT LEAST.

GUESS HE'S BACK ON THE MARKET.

THAT'S NOT—

FOR GOODNESS SAKE, *JAZZ!* WHAT I WAS *GOING* TO SAY IS, IT SOUNDS LIKE HE WAS BEING A JERK . . .

...AND, GOOD FOR YOU. FOR, Y'KNOW, STICKING TO YOUR CHOICES AND... YEAH.

OH.

THANKS, BECKY.

S'OKAY.

SO YEAH, JAKE WAS ACTUALLY RIGHT THERE.

...BUT DON'T TELL HIM THAT! HER VERSION WAS THAT I DITCHED HER WHEN I GOT ALL "BOOKISH AND SNOBBY"!

ha!

SO, YOU THINK YOU'LL BE FRIENDS AGAIN?

UH, I DOUBT IT. WE HAVE NOTHING IN COMMON!

BESIDES, WHO WOULD I TRADE INSULTS WITH THEN?

...I HAVE TO SAY, I AM LOOKING FORWARD TO GETTING HOME FOR CHRISTMAS. GETTING AWAY A BIT.

...A TAMMY WHO SPEAKS HER MIND...

IT WOULD BE GOOD TO EXPRES MYSELF MORE. OPEN UP.

I DO REALLY LIKE HIM...BUT IT'S ONLY HALF ABOUT THAT, REALLY.

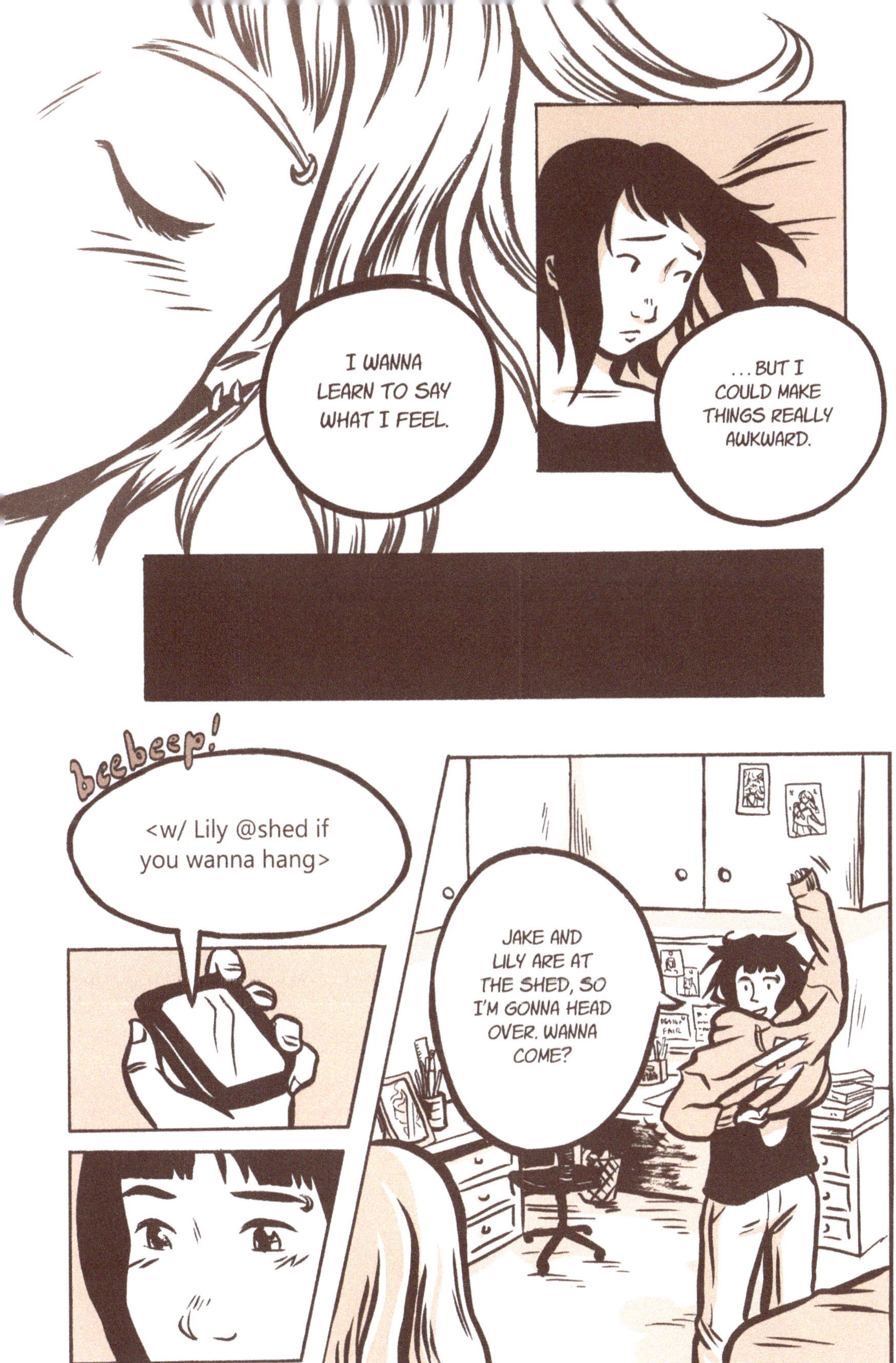
I WANNA LEARN TO SAY WHAT I FEEL.
. . . BUT I COULD MAKE THINGS REALLY AWKWARD.
beebeep!
<w/ Lily @shed if you wanna hang>
JAKE AND LILY ARE AT THE SHED, SO I'M GONNA HEAD OVER. WANNA COME?

NAH, I THINK I'LL STAY HERE FOR A BIT.

SURE.

EAGLE HALL

OH! THAT WAS RYAN!

WHAT'S HE DOING HERE?

...IT'S FINE, TAMMY. SHE KNOWS HER MIND. SHE'LL BE FINE.

KNOCK!

I FOUND THIS DRAWING I DID IN THE SUMMER, AND PUT IT NEXT TO SOMETHING NEW.

AND IT REALLY WAS BETTER - THE NEW ONE - LIKE, A LOT BETTER.

I KIND OF FEEL LIKE I'M ACTUALLY GETTING SOMEWHERE.

I MEAN, I KNOW THERE'S A LONG WAY TO GO, BUT STILL...

Y'KNOW?

YEAH, I KNOW WHAT YOU MEAN.

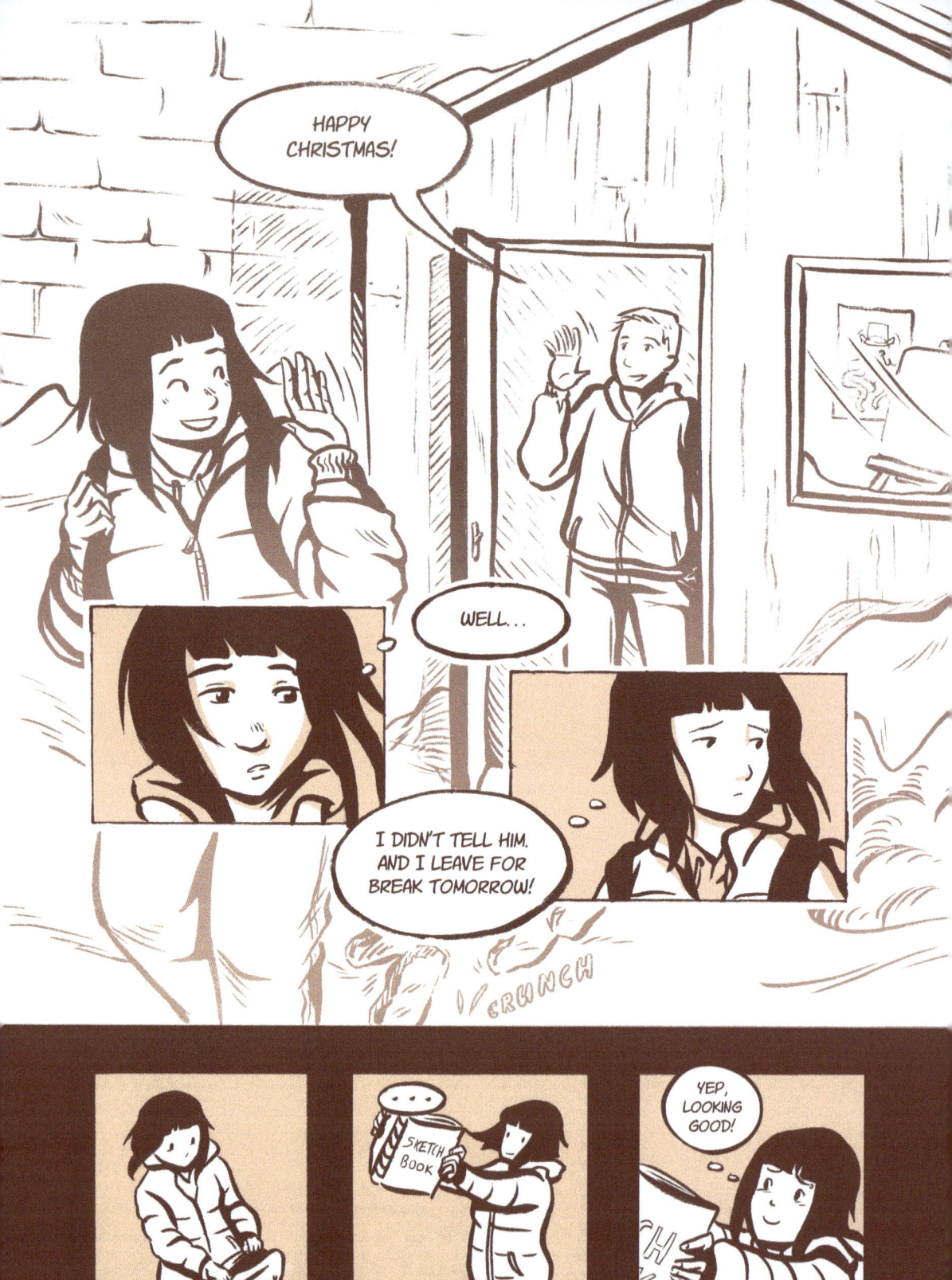

HMM

UM, I WAS WONDERING... WOULD YOU GUYS MIND GETTING A COFFEE IN THE CAF FOR A MINUTE? THERE'S SOMETHING I JUST WANT TO DO QUICK, BEFORE WE GO.

UH, SURE HONEY.

WILL YOU BE HERE FOR A BIT?

YEAH, I'LL BE HERE. WHAT ARE YOU-

YEAH?

WELL, GOOD.

YEAH!

SO.

I'M GETTING PICKED UP SUNDAY. CALL ME WHEN WE'RE BACK IN VANCOUVER SO WE CAN HANG OUT, OKAY?

DEFINITELY.

OH, IT WAS FINE.

I MEAN, SCHOOL'S SCHOOL, Y'KNOW?

AUTHOR'S CORNER

Thanks for reading this book!

This book is both a bit special and a bit odd for me, due to its process...

In the end, it's been a bit like collaborating with past versions of myself.

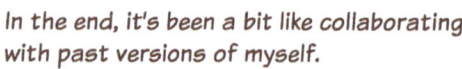

UNDERGRAD SALLY

Just started making comics

POSTGRAD SALLY

Just started freelancing in comics/illustration

I started thinking about it in university, and the first ideas looked like *this*. (Yeah, the curly hair and glasses for Tammy were way too self-insert-y looking!)

Also, drawing ability... er, yeah.

Hey!

Sorry, Undergrad Sally.

I moved to England after my BFA. Soon after, while testing the look of sketches on a painted ground, I did this one. It immediately felt like a good design for Tammy.

Over my first year in the UK, I did a lot of shorter comics, got stuck into UK conventions and competitions, got involved in a comics circle. When I'd been here a year, I heard Markosia were looking for manga-influenced comics.

Like many of my peers, I started out heavily influenced by manga. Since then, time, experience, and wider reading have helped sift out the core influences I took from it - pacing, layouts, sense of place, range of stories - rather than the strong stylistic influence I'd started with.

So Harry Markos and I met, agreed to develop Atomic Sheep, and I got started!

And then. . . life. Work. I was doing an MA. I got married. I started freelancing.

I worked on it in spurts over the next few years, each one developing it a bit more.

And we change, develop, not just in skills... but in interests, ideas, preoccupations.

I read an interview once with an author who mentioned, in regards to a previous novel, that he couldn't have written it now. Not wouldn't, *couldn't*. That struck me. What you create is a product of who you are at that time. Current Me, who was finishing this book, likely wouldn't have written it - or would have done so differently if she had. Because she's not quite the same person, in the same place.

click!

It really was like collaborating with another person on their story... only the other person was a prior version of myself.

Uh, what were you going for here?

Well, I was thinking...

Atomic Sheep isn't autobiographical. But the story certainly developed, while I was in university, from things I was thinking through at the time. I was working on myself, trying to become the sort of person I wanted to be. I gave myself goals, periods of working on something specific - including being less sarcastic, and being more open about my thoughts and feelings!

So I plugged away at this in bits over the years, between lots of other things, all the time developing and changing and coming back to it slightly different each time.

...and *better*, obviously. Plenty of pages needed flat-out redrawing. Others needed touch-ups because when I'd started it, I'd just drawn on printer paper and the ink feathered, and I hadn't scanned at high enough resolution!

What needs redrawing and what doesn't?! I've got to stop somewhere!

"When is a book done?" is kind of a trick question.

And honestly, that's probably something I'll have with every book I ever do. Just, hopefully, to a lesser extent!

This book really belongs to a younger version of myself (and anyone who feels a bit like her). I'm glad I got to finish it for her.

Sally was born in South Africa, and after a stint in Canada now lives in the UK, where she freelances by day and creates stories by night.

Her work has appeared in publications from IDW, Image Comics, Imagine Publications, and more, as well as various self-published works.

Atomic Sheep is her first full-length comic, and its recipe included chocolate, ink, memories of teenage manga discovery, pictures of sloths on the internet, sleep loss, and the experience of having been to eight different schools before university.

You can find more of her work at:

www.sallyjanethompson.co.uk

~

Dedicated to Harry and Lee Thompson, who never asked me to be anything but myself.

~

With many thanks to: Peter, always and for everything; Harry Markos and Sara Westrop; all the lovely comic friends who've provided conversations about craft that have pinged around in my head long afterwards, and who've offered their feedback and brains and encouragement; you , for reading this book!

This book was lettered with Komika Slim and Komika Text, by Apostrophic Labs.
Cover credit uses Comic Andy by Andrew Polhill

Artwork was pencilled with Prismacolour Col-Erase Blue pencils and Pentel Blue 0.5 lead, and inked primarily with a Pentel Pocketbrush, with backup from Muji Calligraphy brushpens, Deleter G-Pen nibs with Windsor and Newton ink, and various fineliners.

 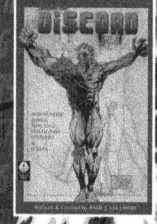

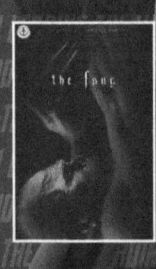

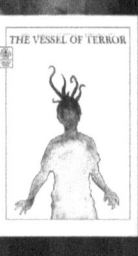